Fit

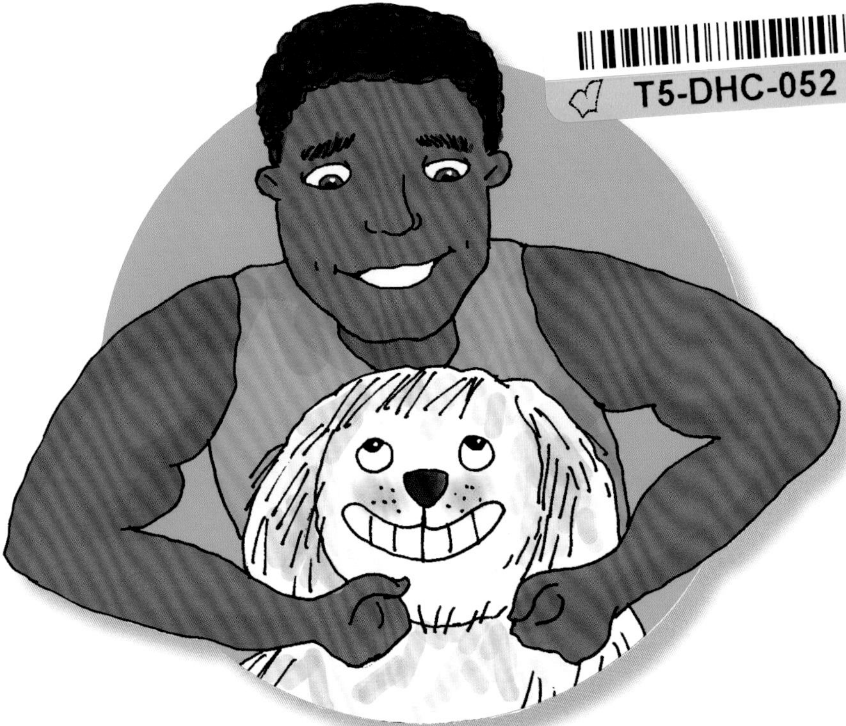

T5-DHC-052

by Susan Hartley • illustrated by Anita DuFalla

Sam is fit.
Fit Sam.

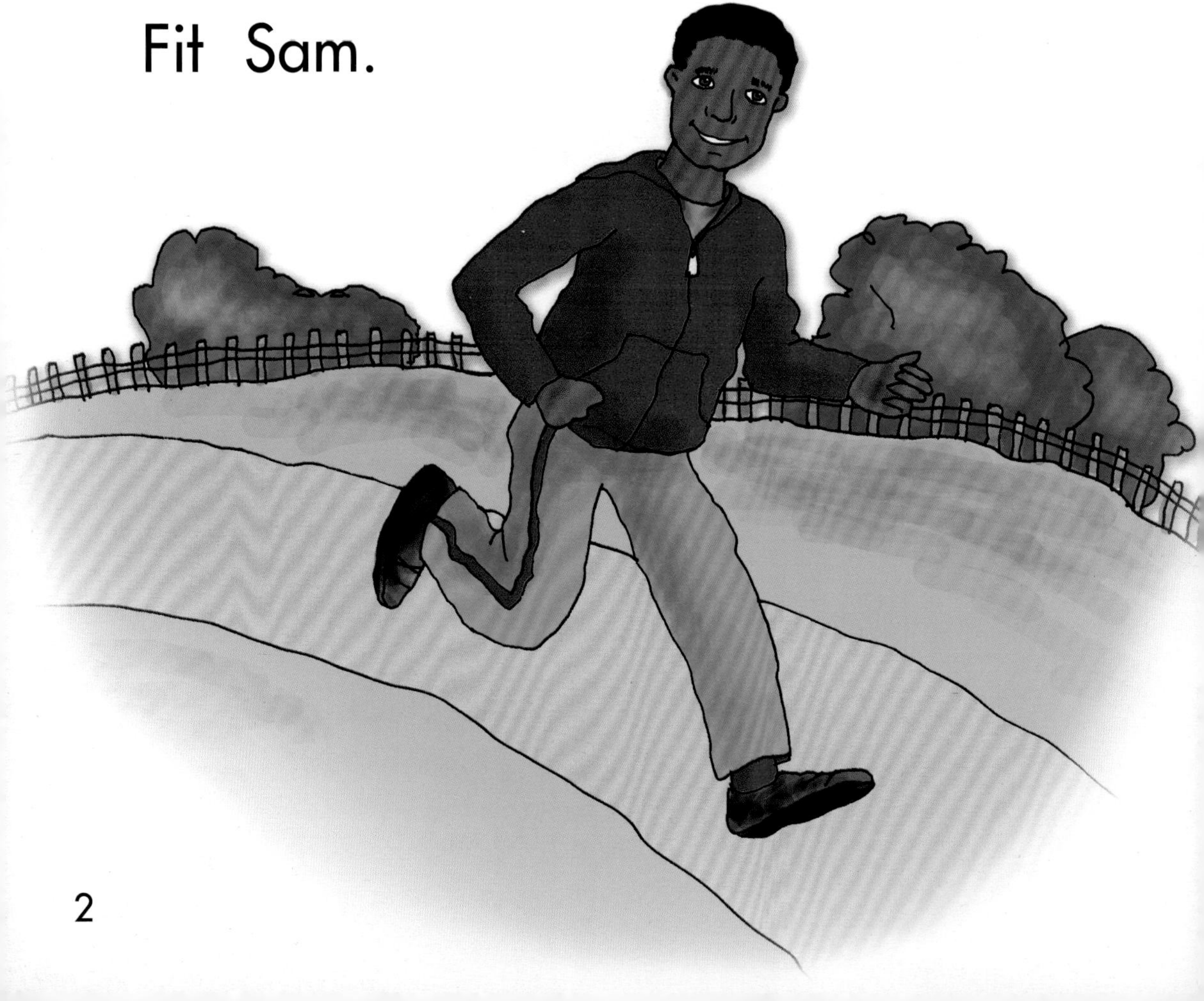

Tim is fit.

Fit Tim.

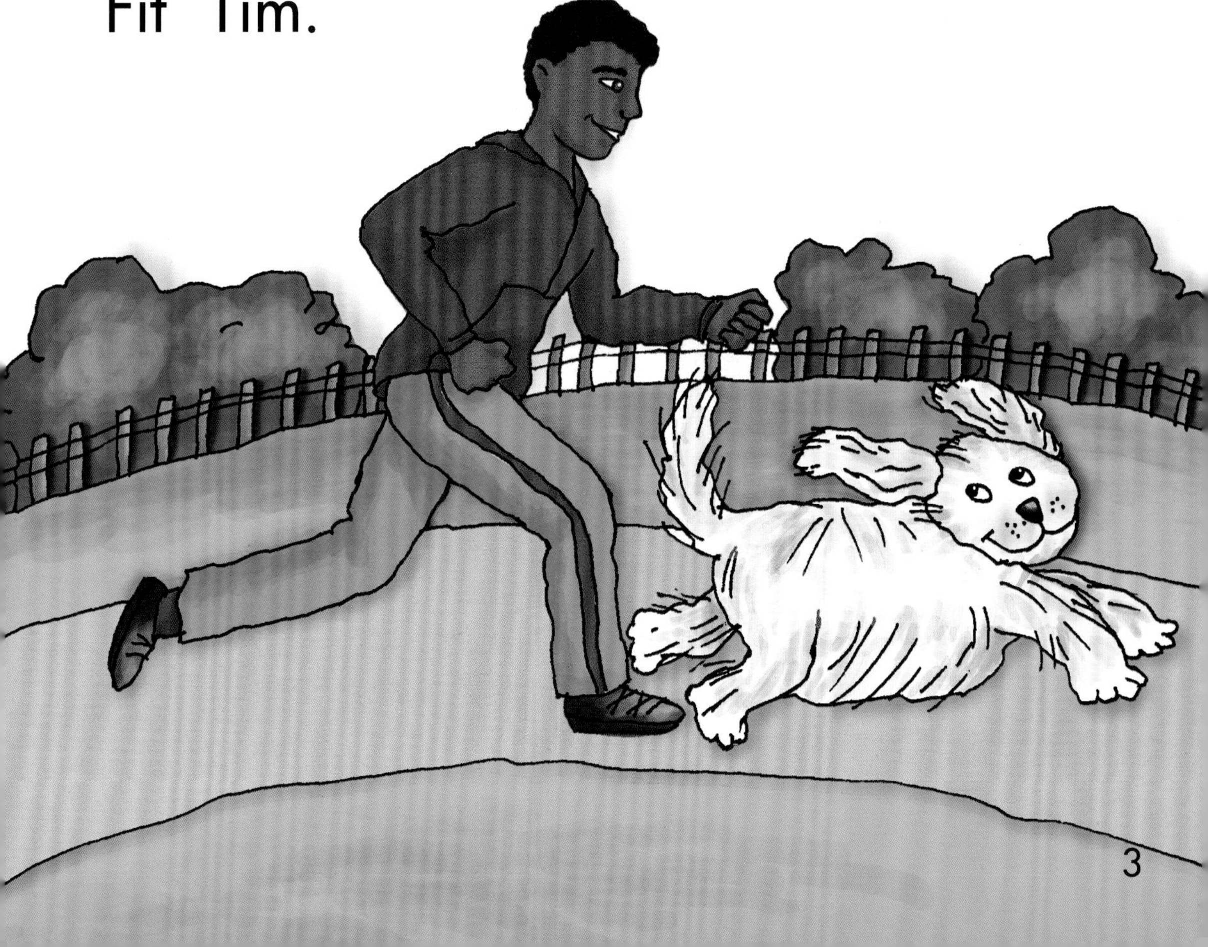

Sam sat.

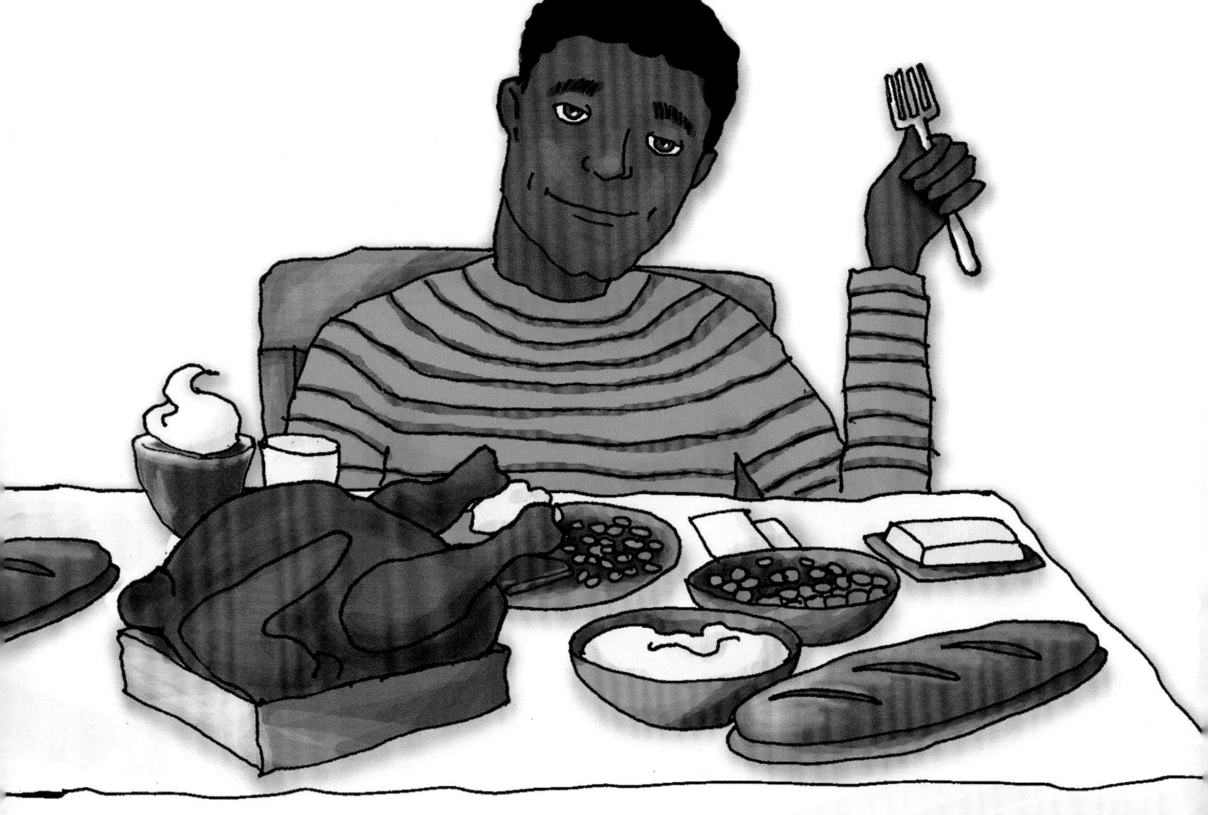

Tim sat.

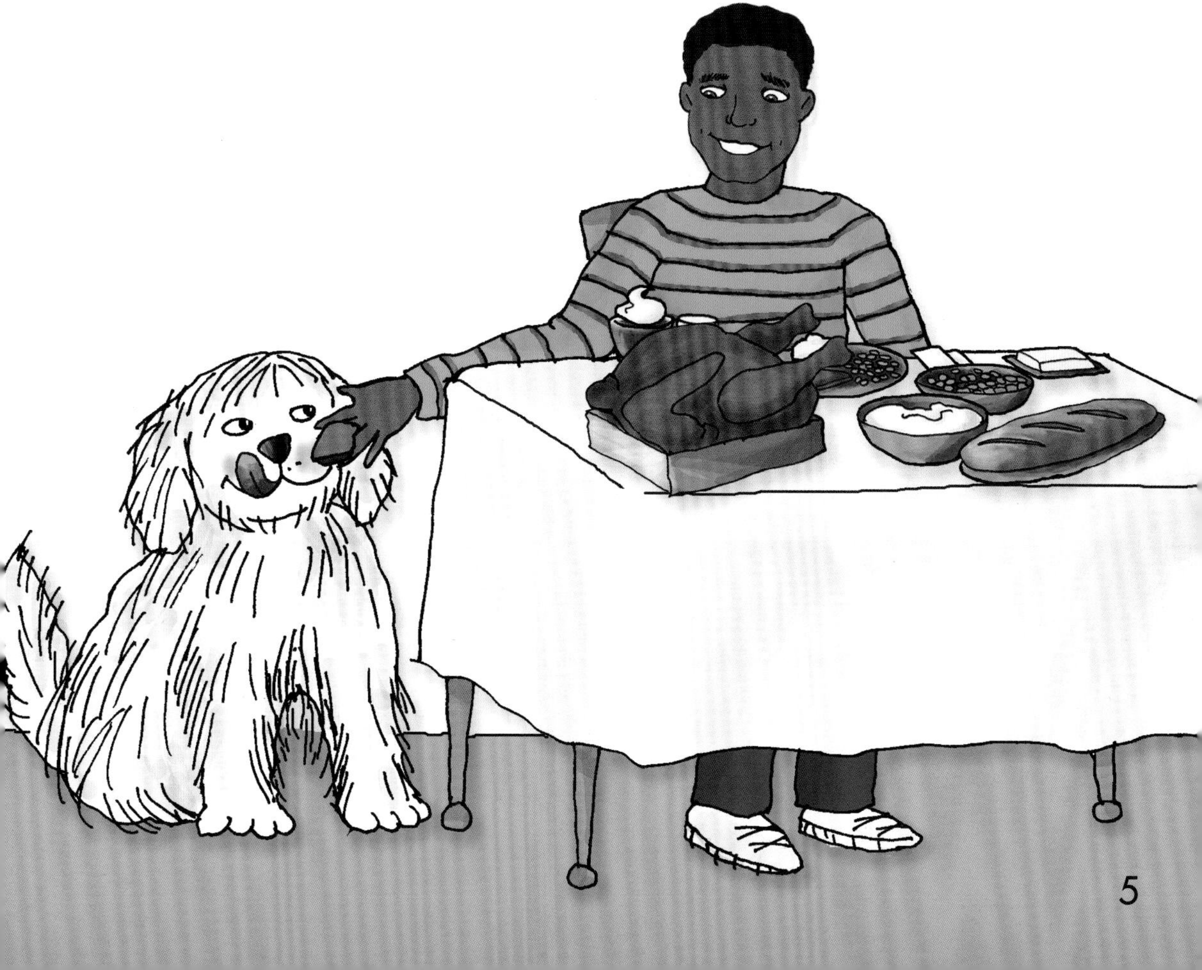

Sam is fat.
Fat Sam!

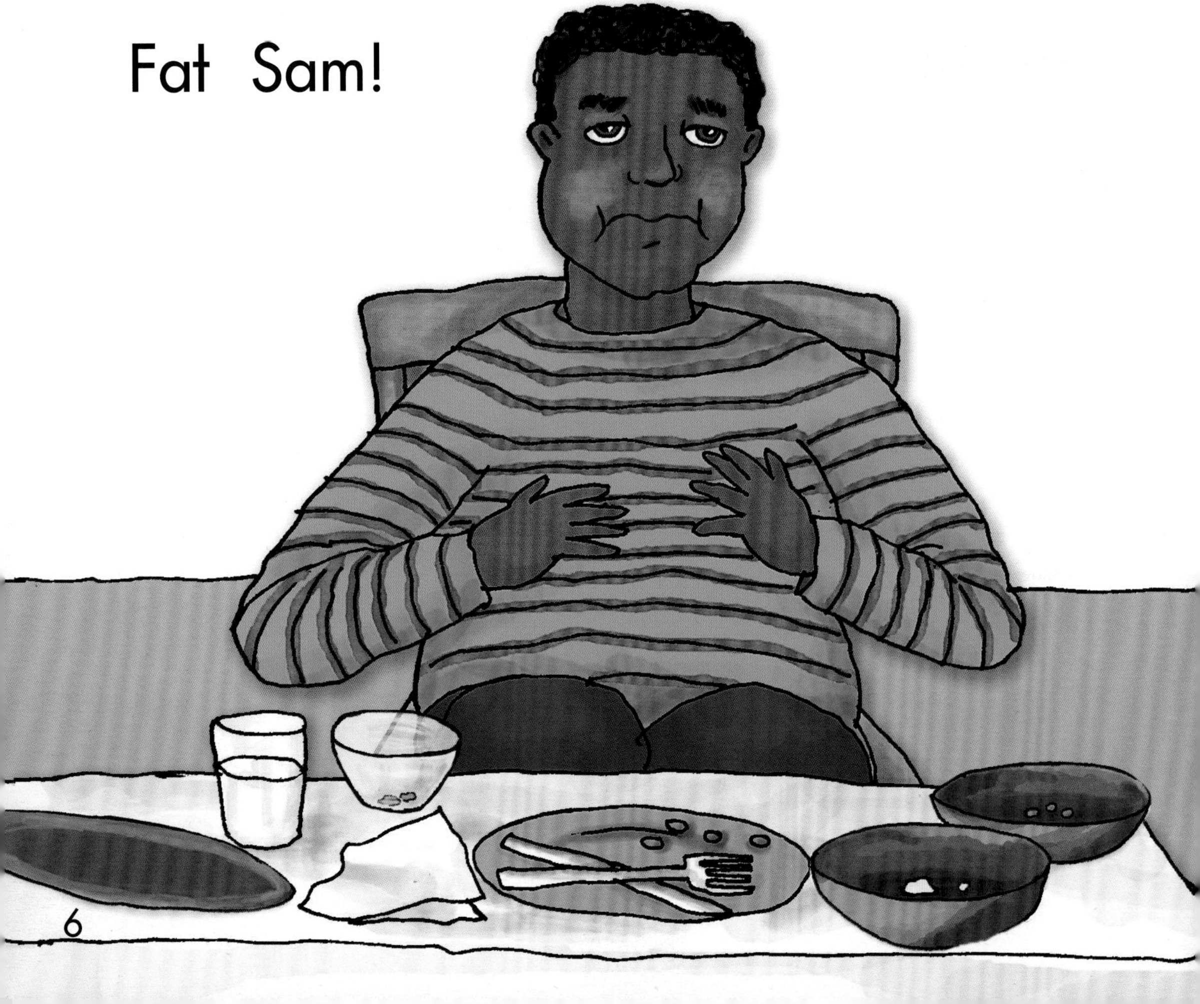

Tim is fat.

Fat Tim!

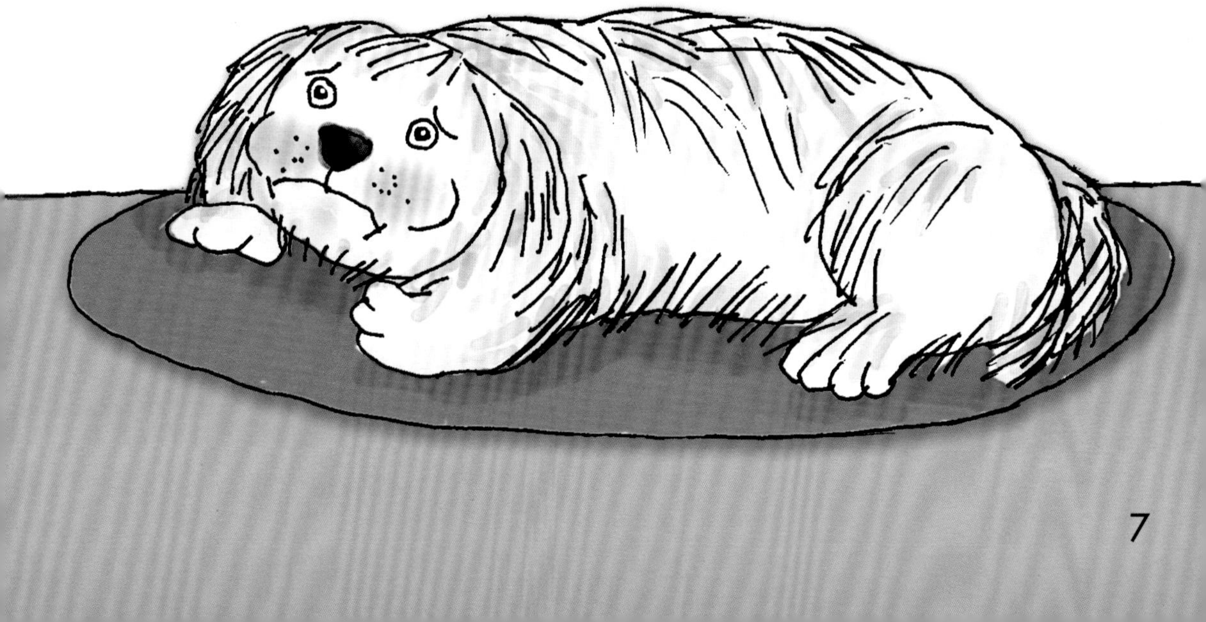

Fan Sam! Fan Tim!

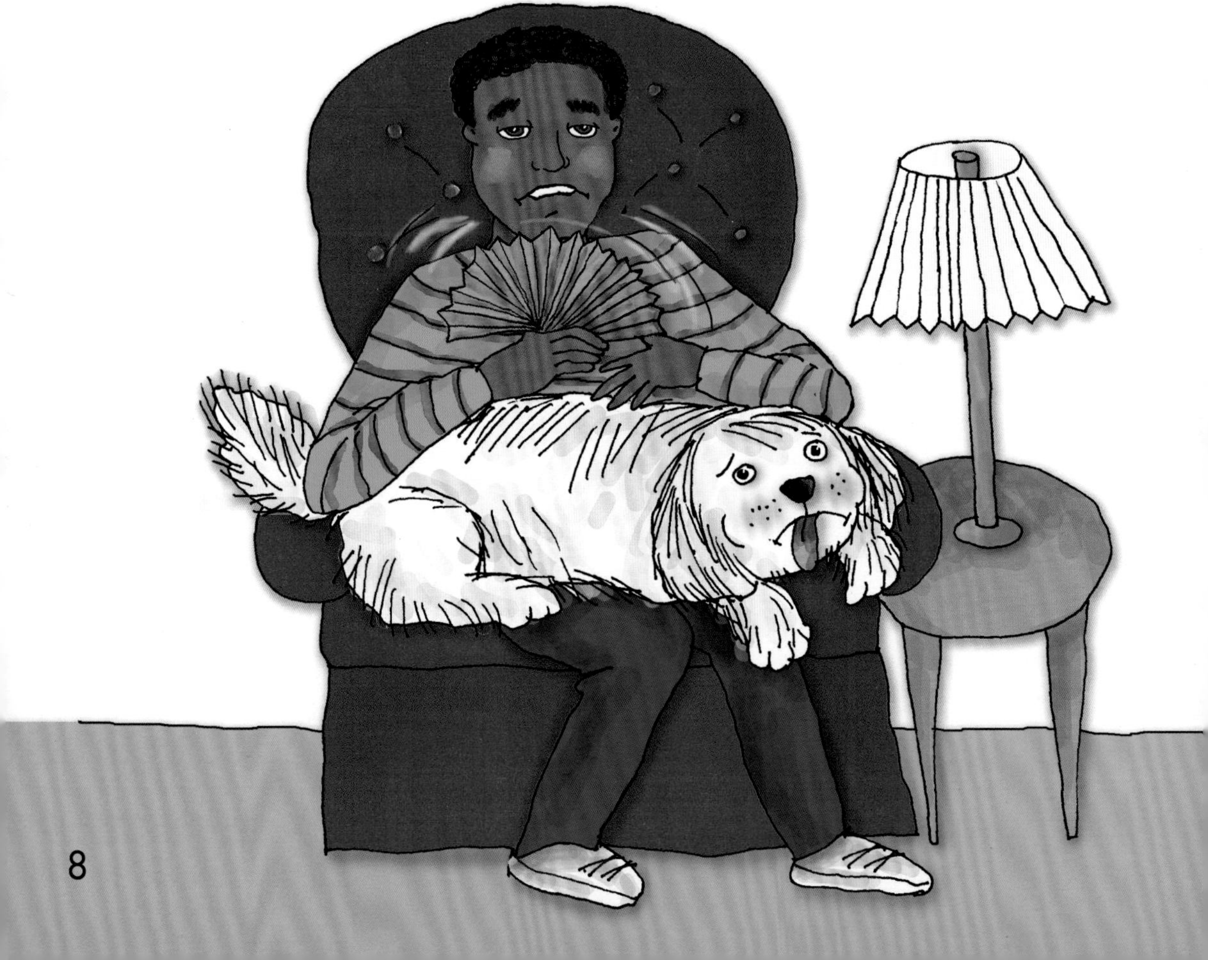